A NOTE TO PARENTS

Reading Aloud with Your Child

Research shows that reading books aloud is the single most valuable support parents can provide in helping children learn to read.

- Be a ham! The more enthusiasm you display, the more your child will enjoy the book.
- Run your finger underneath the words as you read to signal that the print carries the story.
- Leave time for examining the illustrations more closely; encourage your child to find things in the pictures.
- Invite your youngster to join in whenever there's a repeated phrase in the text.
- Link up events in the book with similar events in your child's life.
- If your child asks a question, stop and answer it. The book can be a means to learning more about your child's thoughts.

Listening to Your Child Read Aloud

The support of your attention and praise is absolutely crucial to your child's continuing efforts to learn to read.

- If your child is learning to read and asks for a word, give it immediately so that the meaning of the story is not interrupted. DO NOT ask your child to sound out the word.
- On the other hand, if your child initiates the act of sounding out, don't intervene.
- If your child is reading along and makes what is called a miscue, listen for the sense of the miscue. If the word "road" is substituted for the word "street," for instance, no meaning is lost. Don't stop the reading for a correction.
- If the miscue makes no sense (for example, "horse" for "house"), ask your child to reread the sentence because you're not sure you understand what's just been read.
- Above all else, enjoy your child's growing command of print and make sure you give lots of praise. *You are your child's first teacher—and the most important one. Praise from you is critical for further risk-taking and learning.*

—Priscilla Lynch
Ph.D., New York University
Educational Consultant

For my mother,
the one and only Bea.
— W.C.L.

Library of Congress Cataloging-in-Publication Data

Lewison, Wendy Cheyette.
    "Buzz," said the bee/by Wendy Cheyette Lewison; illustrated by Hans Wilhelm.
        p.   cm.—(Hello reader)
    "Level 1."
    Summary: As one animal sits on another in an accumulating progression, the reader learns the sounds each animal makes.
    ISBN 0-590-44185-X
    [1. Animal sounds—Fiction.] I. Wilhelm, Hans, 1945–   ill.
II. Title. III. Series.
PZ7.L5884Bu   1992
[E]—dc20   91-19610
                                                                CIP
                                                                AC

24 23 22   67/9

Printed in the U.S.A.   23
First Scholastic printing, March 1992

BUZZZZZZZZZ

Said the Bee

by Wendy Cheyette Lewison
Illustrated by Hans Wilhelm

Hello Reader! — Level 1

Scholastic Inc.
New York   Toronto   London   Auckland   Sydney

Once there was a bee who sat on a duck.

"QUACK," said the duck.
"There's a bee on me."
And the duck said, "Scat,"
but the bee just sat.

So the duck quacked again

and sat on a hen.

"CLUCK," said the hen.
"There's a duck on me."
And the hen said, "Scat,"
but the duck just sat.

So the hen danced a jig

and sat on a pig.

"OINK," said the pig.
"There's a hen on me."
And the pig said, "Scat,"
but the hen just sat.

So the pig took a bow

and sat on a cow.

"MOO," said the cow.
"There's a pig on me."
And the cow said, "Scat,"
but the pig just sat.

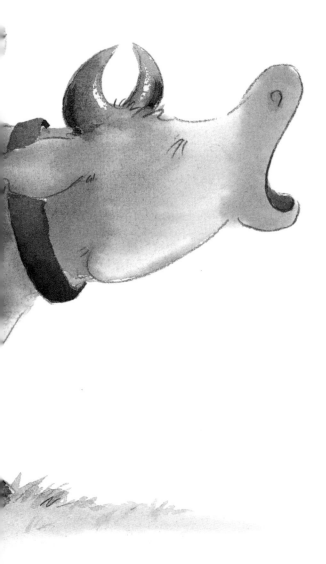

The cow began to weep

and sat on a sheep
who was fast asleep.

So the cow said, "MOO,"

and the pig said, "OINK,"

and the hen said, "CLUCK,"

and the duck said, "QUACK."

Then the bee said,
"BUZZ-Z-Z-Z!"

And that's all there was.